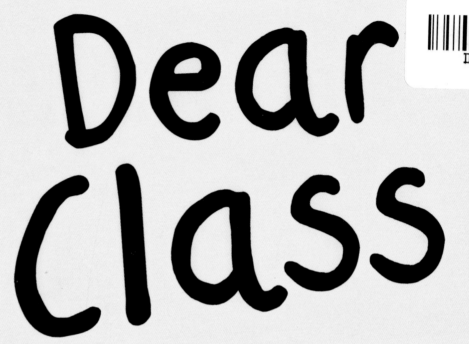

Dear Class

By Amy Husband

Published by Albury Books in 2016
Albury Court, Albury, Thame, OX9 2LP, United Kingdom

Sales and Enquiries:
Kuperard Publishers and Distributors
59 Hutton Grove, London, N12 8DS
Tel: +44 (0) 208 446 2440
Fax: +44 (0) 208 446 2441
sales@kuperard.co.uk | www.kuperard.co.uk

Text © Amy Husband | Illustrations © Amy Husband
The rights of Amy Husband to be identified as the
author and illustrator have been
asserted by them in accordance with
the Copyright, Designs and Patents Act, 1988

ISBN 978-1-910571-48-4 (paperback)

A CIP catalogue record for this book is available from
the British Library
10 9 8 7 6 5 4 3
Printed in the United Kingdom

Albury Children's

For my
sister, Nicki
A.H.

Dragon Class
Sunnybank Primary School

Dear Dragon Class,

This is the start of a very special week. On Friday, we break up for the summer. It's holiday time for our pet rabbit, Boris, too and one lucky person will get to take him home and look after him all summer.

Please write a letter telling me why you should be the one to take Boris home. I will then decide who will be best at caring for Boris.

When writing your letter, remember to:

1. Write your address at the top of your letter.
2. Start with the greeting "Dear" followed by the addressee's name.
3. Start a new paragraph for each new subject.
4. Close the letter with a suitable ending.

Remember, it's especially important to be on your best behaviour this week. Good luck, everyone!

Yours sincerely,

C Brooks

Miss C. Brooks

The (Best) Table,
Dragon Class,
Sunnybank Primary School

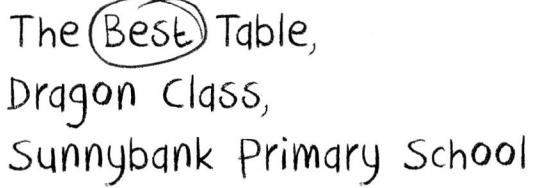

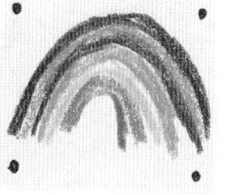
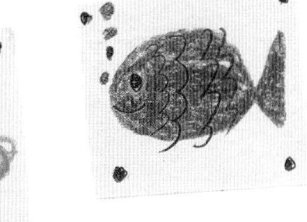

BORIS

Dear Michael,

I see you're writing a letter. I bet you're trying to get to take Boris home this summer.

But you'll never win, because:

1. You're in trouble for breaking your chair yesterday. 2. It's your fault I laughed and got moved, so you're in double ~~truble~~ trouble. 3. Bruno would HATE Boris.

So you should give up and help me write my letter instead, because I've got a much better chance of winning.

Yours sincerely,

Nicholas

P.S. I'm going to ask Molly to pass you this letter.

Pass your own letters! Molly

PLEASE, Molly, this is a matter of life and death. Nicholas

Dear Nicholas,

No, I won't help you write your letter. Write your own! It's your fault you got told off. I broke the chair by accident, you're the one who laughed and sprayed water all over Molly's maths book.

Anyway, I'd be <u>LOADS</u> better than you at looking after Boris because:

1. Bruno would <u>LOVE</u> Boris and they could keep each other company.
2. I have loads of experience with animals.
3. I don't spit water everywhere when I laugh.

Yours insultedly,

Michael

My maths book is still damp, actually, so pass your own letters. Molly

Just pass the letter! Michael

Boris would get triple-layered carrot cake with icing every day!

The Most <u>Amazing</u> Table
In The School, Dragon Class,
Sunnybank Primary School

Dear Michael,

FINE, I'll write my own letter.
I had lots of cool plans for the
summer, but I guess you and
Bruno won't want to join me if
you think I spit water everywhere!
Oh well, I'm sure Molly will
invite you and Bruno to ALL
her dolls' tea parties instead.

Yours <u>offendedly</u>,
Nicholas

I wouldn't invite either of you to anything. Molly

Boris would get carrot pie and lettuce soup for lunch.

The Most Amazing Table
In The Country, Dragon Class,
Sunnybank Primary School

Dear Nicholas,

I don't like dolls' tea parties. And I had loads of great plans for ~~the~~ the holidays too. Me and Bruno were going to go on a massive bike ride up the river to the waterfalls with Boris in a basket! I guess you won't want to join us if you're still cross with me?

Yours disappointedly,

Michael

What's wrong with dolls' tea parties? Molly

BAT CAVES

For breakfast, Boris would get scrambled carrots on toast with lettuce fries, grass ice cream and garlic slugs.

The <u>Best</u> Table In The World, Dragon Class,
Sunnybank Primary School

Dear Michael,

I don't like dolls' tea parties either. The bike ride sounds brilliant, but Boris and I had even better plans. We were going to have a Pets vs Humans football match in my garden. Do you want to come?

Yours hopefully,
Nicholas

Do I look like a postman? Molly

Yes. Nicholas

You are SO annoying. Molly

Just deliver the letter! Nicholas

What did your last slave die of? Molly

Answering back. Nicholas

For tea, Boris could have carrot scones with creamed ants and blackberry jam. ⟶

The Table That Would Be Even More Brilliant If My **Best Friend** Was On It, Dragon Class, Sunnybank Primary School

Dear Nicholas,

The Pets vs Humans football match in your garden sounds fantastic. Bruno would love it! And we could build the best, biggest-ever tree house in my garden.

 Yours excitedly,

Michael

P.S. Does this mean we're friends again?
P.P.S. I'm sure Bruno will let Boris share his food.

For a snack, what about stewed cucumber with wormy custard and garlic slugs? ⟶

The Table That Would Be
The Best If Me And My Best
Friend Were On It Together,
Dragon Class,
Sunnybank Primary School

Dear Michael,

Yes we are definitely friends
again. I really want to build the
best, biggest-ever tree house!
And how about going on a balloon ride?
Boris and Bruno could be the first ever rabbit and
dog duo to travel the globe in a hot air balloon!

Yours happily,
Nicholas

Dear Michael
and Nicholas,
I'm not passing any
more notes for anyone!
Yours sincerely,
Molly

Mmm - grass chow
mein with spider rice
for dinner!

The  Brainiest Table Ever,
Dragon Class,
Sunnybank Primary School

Dear Nicholas,

I've had a brainwave!
Shall I write a letter
to Miss Brooks from both
of us? Best friends would
be DOUBLE BRILLIANT
at looking after Boris.
He would have twice
as much fun with
two of us!

Yours brainily,
Michael

Dear Michael,

Yes, definitely! Thanks for writing the letter, you're the best friend EVER.

Yours gratefully,
Nicholas

Nicholas and Michael – SEE ME.

Miss Brooks

Dragon Class
Sunnybank Primary School

Dear Michael and Nicholas,

Thank you for your letter. It was very interesting to read about the things you would do with Boris if you were allowed to take him home.

Despite your being naughty and writing letters during class, I was impressed that you addressed your letters ⁱ'ⁱ Also, I think that looking after Boris would teach you:

- Responsibility
- Respect
- Nutrition

So I have decided that both of you will look after Boris over the holidays. I am sure that you will take good care of him.

Yours optimistically,

Miss C. Brooks

P.S. I notice you've been discussing what you would feed Boris –
maybe we should have a little chat about what rabbits eat.
I'm not sure they like wormy custard!

Dear Michael and Nicholas,

What a brilliant holiday! I really
enjoyed the rabbit fairground rides
you made in the garden. Bruno
made a great bucking bronco.
I really hope I can spend my
holiday with you again
next time.

Yours hungrily,
Boris

P.S. It turns out that
I shouldn't have eaten
so many carrots before
going on the rides.
No wonder I got
the hiccups.